A HIDDEN JAM

RAISED AND GLAZED COZY MYSTERIES, BOOK 9

EMMA AINSLEY

SUMMER PRESCOTT BOOKS PUBLISHING

CHAPTER ONE

"It's the back door," Maggie Sharpe said into the cell phone she held to her ear. She sat in her car with the doors locked, parked in the alley behind her shop, Dogwood Donuts. It was barely after midnight. The alarm had gone off a few minutes before, alerting both Maggie and her best friend and business partner, Ruby Cobb, that something was wrong.

Living just about a block away, Maggie elected to drive down and check things out for herself. When she did, the first thing she saw was the back door standing wide open.

"You ought to call the police," Ruby told her. "And whatever you do, wait for them to show up before you go traipsing around trying to figure out what happened."

"Hanging up to call the police now," Maggie said. She made no other promises.

Within three minutes, an officer from the Dogwood Mountain Police Department was on the scene. Maggie recognized the young officer, though she was unsure of her name. She quickly introduced herself as Officer Ruiz before she pulled out her flashlight and unsnapped her gun holster as she walked inside. She flipped the lights on when she reached the switch. Maggie stood at the doorway, ten feet closer than the officer had instructed, and waited for news.

"Ms. Sharpe," Officer Ruiz called a few minutes after she had gone through the swinging door that led to the front of the business. "I need you to come up here and take a look at this."

Maggie walked carefully through the open door. She hugged her arms around her middle. Despite the heat being on in the shop, she felt an unmistakable chill in the air. "What's going on?" she asked as she made her way through the kitchen.

The officer didn't have to explain. As soon as Maggie saw the condition of the front counter she knew that the donut shop had, indeed, been burglarized. "Looks like they broke the glass on the front doors as well as the lock in the back," the officer announced. "I know this is a shock, but I'm going to need for you to check things out and make a list of everything that is damaged or missing."

"Did you check to make sure no one was in here?" Maggie asked, her head on a swivel.

"I did. We are the only two in the building," the officer assured her.

Maggie surveyed the front counter. Several items had been pulled from the shelves below. The floor was littered with broken ceramic coffee cups. "I think we better go check in the office and in the cooler."

Officer Ruiz reached her hand out and placed it on Maggie's arm. "I've checked in both places already."

"Okay, but I keep the iPad in the office when we lock up for the night and any extra cash on hand is kept in a small bank bag on the top shelf of the cooler in the back. I'm sure you didn't check for those."

"I didn't." She tilted her head to the side and spoke into the radio pinned to her lapel. "Officer Ruiz requesting backup at Dogwood Donuts," she said. "Possible burglary. No suspects present."

"You need backup?" Maggie chose not to comment on how she'd only referred to it as a possible burglary when it was clear that's exactly what it was.

Officer Ruiz nodded. "We're going to process this

scene for anything we can find. This is the second robbery in town in the last two days. The thieves seem to be targeting businesses overnight. The flower shop downtown was hit around ten last night."

Maggie dropped her shoulders. "I suspect this means we're closed for the day."

Officer Ruiz smiled. "I was going to mention that, yes, but I was also hoping we could take a walk over to the food truck soon and rule out any break-in there. That way you can at least run a part of your business if everything looks okay."

The idea surprised her. She hadn't even considered the food truck. "Thanks for the reminder," she said. "That's actually a great suggestion. We'll have a partial business day at least." They wouldn't be able to do quite as much with the lunch boxes from the food truck, but something was better than nothing. As long as the truck was clear, of course. She sent a quick text to Ruby to tell her what had happened and to let her know about the food truck idea.

"Oh, trust me." Officer Ruiz turned to her and grinned as they walked back through the kitchen toward the cooler. "My suggestion was entirely self-serving. I don't want to face the rest of my shift without one of your maple lattes or a chocolate donut.

Chief Mission treats us too often. I think I might be addicted."

Maggie soaked in the compliment and led the officer to the cooler. She wanted to thank her for the distraction while they assessed the damage done by an intruder. It helped to set her nerves at ease before they took a look to see what might be missing.

When she opened the door to the cooler, it was clear that the thief had known what to look for. The floor was littered with overturned food containers. Maggie searched carefully along the top shelf for the bag. "It's gone," she said when she found the container. "The thief knew enough to locate the bank bag we use for petty cash."

Officer Ruiz began making notes in her small notepad. "How much do you keep in the bag?"

"About five hundred," Maggie said. "We use petty cash for quick runs to the grocery store for ingredients we run out of, and that sort of thing."

"Let's leave this as it is for now. We need to take a look at the office as well. If it's the same thief from the flower shop, I'm afraid you might be missing more than just cash."

Maggie frowned and stepped carefully around the mess on the floor. She led Officer Ruiz to the small office in the back of the kitchen. The door appeared to have been kicked in.

"I don't even lock the door," Maggie said and shook her head. "They didn't have to destroy it."

"Go ahead and check for the iPad," Officer Ruiz said. "I just heard another car pull up. They can begin processing the scene for evidence while we go out and check on the food truck. After that, you can look around further for anything else that might be missing that isn't as obvious."

Maggie opened the desk drawer where she kept the iPad used for sales at the front counter. "It's gone, too," she announced.

"Ruiz," a voice called from the kitchen. Maggie knew right away that the call about the donut shop had reached the chief of police himself. "What's going on around here?" Chief Brett Mission appeared in the doorway.

"I will give you a full report in a sec, Chief," Officer Ruiz said. "Right now, we're going to check out the status of the food truck in the front."

Brett nodded. He gazed at Maggie for an extra-long moment. "We're going to get to the bottom of this, Maggie," he said quietly. "I promise."

She smiled weakly and nodded. She desperately wanted to fall into his arms and let him hug her worries away, but somehow, it didn't feel like the right time for that.

Maggie waited while the officer handed her notepad over to the chief. Then she allowed herself to be led out the back door and into the darkness. They walked slowly around the side of the building while the officer shined her flashlight on the side of the building. "Do you have the keys to the food truck?" Officer Ruiz asked her when they reached the parking lot in the front.

She nodded and pulled her keys from the pocket of her jeans. She had taken a moment to slip her regular clothes on when she got the alert on her cell phone from the alarm. "I have them," she said, thankful she kept the food truck key on her regular key ring.

"Well, let's wait a second and let me have a look around the exterior first," Ruiz said. She pointed the flashlight toward the truck's windshield. "I'm sure whoever was here is long gone now, but it's always better to be cautious."

Maggie followed her around the truck, even though she was sure that's not what the officer had wanted. She exhaled at last when it appeared that the burglar had skipped the vehicle. "Everything looks normal," she said when she unlocked the back doors and led the officer inside. They moved through the truck, opening the door to the small bathroom, and checking for the smaller iPad she kept hidden beneath the automatic mini donut machine. "I think we're good here." She sent another text to Ruby, letting her know the food truck would be their means of operation for the day.

Officer Ruiz looked at Maggie as her fingers flew over the keyboard. "Alright. Let's head back inside and I'll take your statement. Then you can get the word out to your staff about the main business closing for the day."

Maggie laughed. "That's what I was just doing. My partner, Ruby, is going to let everyone know. But I do need to figure out a plan of action for the food truck."

"So, no running back home for a bit more sleep before you open in a few hours, then?" Officer Ruiz asked as they walked back around the other side of the building toward the back.

She shook her head. "No way I'll be going back to sleep tonight."

CHAPTER TWO

Maggie started her day trying to be as positive as possible and absolutely refused to outwardly show her concern about what went on at the donut shop. It was bad enough that someone had broken in at all, never mind the fact that whoever it was had known exactly where to find what they were looking for. The only people that knew where she kept the petty cash bag and the iPads, were her employees. But she knew them. She knew they wouldn't do something like that and that all any of them had to do was ask and she'd give them the shirt off her back. She was banking on the fact that the police would find something to prove who it was or at least who it wasn't. Her employees were also her friends, and they deserved the benefit of the doubt, if nothing else.

"What happened last night?" Myra Sawyer asked Maggie when she arrived at work a few hours later.

"The donut shop got robbed, or haven't you heard," Orson Hawley grumbled and moved past her. He picked up a to-go order and headed back toward the parking lot. Since he arrived for work, he'd worked to organize the orders, car-hop style. Maggie was impressed at his forethought, but Orson let his normal grumpiness shine through.

"Somebody woke up in a mood," Ruby observed. "Was he acting like this last night?"

Myra shrugged. "I don't know. Brooks took me out to a movie and Orson was supposed to have been out on a date with Gretchen, but instead, he was in bed when I got home," she said. Since her arrival to Dogwood Mountain, Myra had gone from being homeless and on the run to renting Orson's extra bedroom and bathroom. The arrangement worked out well for the both of them, despite Orson's gruff nature.

When Maggie first met him, she'd seen him as an entitled and grumpy older man who expected a hand-out. Though things had changed quickly after she'd hired him at the donut shop. Orson was still grumpy but had become a hard-working member of the Dogwood Donuts staff and part of her family. To hear that he might be having a hard time in his relationship with Gretchen LeClair, the owner of the local bed and breakfast, hurt her heart.

"I sure hope nothing happened between him and Gretchen," Maggie whispered. She moved around Ruby to mix the batter for a new round of donuts. "I know they like to keep their relationship private, but I can't help but be curious."

Myra promised she'd keep a close eye on Orson as she swirled whipped cream over a vanilla latte for the next order.

"I wish they'd get on with it inside so we can get back to business as usual," Ruby said. "We could all be in the best times of our lives but having an upset at work like this is enough to drive anyone crazy."

"Brooks said that they are gathering as much evidence as they can find," Myra said. Brooks Macklin had risen quickly in the ranks at the local police station. Although they had not officially declared anything, Myra and Brooks had become a sweet couple nearly as soon as they met. "Apparently we weren't the only place hit last night."

"What? You mentioned the flower shop, but I thought you said it was the night before?" Ruby turned to Maggie. "Who else was hit?"

"An Italian restaurant and a gas station out on the

highway," Myra answered. "Brooks said whoever is doing it, if it's the same person, isn't leaving much evidence behind."

"That's just terrific," Maggie said, feeling upset but a little more confident in the fact that one of the people who worked with her had not suddenly decided to begin a life of crime and rob all the local businesses in the area.

Ruby handed the coffee Myra had made out to a waiting customer at the window closest to her and turned back to Maggie. "Did the alert wake Bradley or Wyatt up last night?"

"Wyatt was already awake," Maggie said with a yawn. Bradley, her son, was on leave from the Navy after an unexpected delivery made him a father. At under a month old, Wyatt was not yet sleeping through the night. Maggie found herself unable to sleep when a baby cried under her roof. It was just one of those things about being a mom.

"Do you think he's sick?" Ruby asked. Childcare was the one thing Maggie knew more about than her best friend. Happily childless in her fifties, Ruby ran a farm, wrote cookbooks, and had a long career as a chef before coming to work at the donut shop.

"I think he's a newborn," Maggie said. "A newborn who may be mixed up between night and day or suffering from colic or maybe he just wants to be held constantly."

"Why so many choices?" Ruby asked.

"Because my son reads books and tries his best to problem solve when it comes to his baby son," Maggie explained. "He tries his best, but he doesn't understand that babies are not problems to be solved. They are babies, and babies wake up and cry at night."

"You sound tired," Myra said. "When does Bradley return to the ship?"

Maggie turned the mini donut machine on and leaned against the counter. "He isn't returning to the ship," she said with a sigh. "He's been transferred to a base in Oklahoma. I don't know what will happen in the long run, but for now, this is the plan."

"There aren't any naval bases in Oklahoma," Orson said. He had returned to the food truck for the next order.

"It's a joint something or other on an Army base I think." Fatigue made it hard for her to find the words to properly understand what was happening. "I offered to keep Wyatt here for a few months while he served out the rest of his deployment, but Bradley is determined. He said his commanding officer helped him map out a different career track, and it's wonderful. There is a great daycare situation on base."

"That sounds like good news," Orson said as he waited. "I think you raised a good man."

"Better get the cinnamon rolls ready," Myra said, quickly changing the subject. She pointed out the window where Brett was making his way to the food truck.

"Good morning," Brett said from the open order window. "I'll just take an order of glazed mini donuts and a coffee."

"You don't want your usual?" Maggie asked. "We made a small batch of cinnamon rolls that we just have to put icing on, and I can easily whip up a cinnamon latte for you."

Brett's eyes widened. "You can? Then yes, absolutely I will take my usual. I just figured with the big kitchen shut down you would be limited."

"Speaking of the big kitchen…" Ruby stuck her head out the window.

"Tomorrow." Brett chuckled. "We should be finished in a couple of hours but by then you'll be getting ready to close anyway. We're just trying our best to gather all the evidence we can, no matter how minuscule."

"I'll be happy to be back in the shop itself tomorrow," Maggie said.

"We'll be right with you," Myra called to the new customers standing just behind Brett.

A young girl walked over to the second window. "Is the donut shop closed or something?" She stood next to a tall, handsome young man. Together, they looked like they belonged on the gym floor of a high school being crowned prom king and queen.

"Temporarily," Ruby replied. "What can we get for you?"

Maggie passed a bag of cinnamon rolls through the other window to Brett, followed by his coffee in a to-go cup. She watched as he turned slowly to the side. His eyes fixed on the young girl. "Layla?"

The girl turned to him and smiled. "Dad!" she exclaimed and threw her arms around him. Maggie cringed as the cinnamon latte sloshed out of the drinking hole in the lid. "I didn't expect to see you!"

"I can say the same," he said. "What are you doing in town? Is school out?"

"No." The girl smiled. She pushed her long brown hair off of her shoulder and smiled brightly. "We decided to just live for a while."

"We?" Brett asked. His eyes traveled to the

smiling young man standing just behind is daughter. "Who is 'we'?"

Layla stepped back and wove her arm through the boy's arm. "Dad, this is Tommy Pogue, my partner," she said. "We've decided to take some time off together."

"Your partner? Do you have classes together or something?" Brett asked.

Maggie almost doubled over from the angst she felt for him. "I don't think she means lab partner, Brett," she said softly.

"No, Dad." Layla sighed. "He's my life partner and we're staying at this super cute bed and breakfast with the funniest name. Dogwood House! Can you believe it? So cute, right?"

"You're staying at the bed and breakfast? You two, together?" Brett shoved his bag back through the open order window and pulled his cell phone from his uniform pocket. "I'm going to have a word with Gretchen about this right now. It isn't legal to rent one room to two underage kids."

"Dad!" Layla shouted. "We are not underage!" She pulled her arm out from around the boy's arm and folded her arms over her chest. "I should have known you would be like this, but if you must know, the owner of the bed and breakfast was very nice to us, and she gave us a discount so we could get two rooms."

"Oh, well." He put his phone back and crossed his arms, still not completely satisfied. "You're going to have to forgive me. You saunter in and announce that you're leaving school and then shove this boy in my face. What does your mother have to say about all of this?"

"Mom happens to support our decision," Layla shot back. "And our relationship, not that it's any of your business. She recognizes that I am almost twenty and capable of making my own choices."

"Layla, you are too young to ditch school and shack up with someone," Brett said. His voice was suddenly husky.

"First off, Dad, it isn't 'ditching school'," she said. "It's like a gap year but in the middle instead of before. We both agreed that it would be good for our mental health and desire to travel the world. And two, we are not shacking up. We are in a committed, non-binding adult relationship with an undetermined future."

Ruby turned to Maggie and mouthed, "Wow."

"I'm sorry. You said a year?" Brett choked on the words. "You think you're going to leave school for an

CHAPTER THREE

By closing time, the police tape had disappeared from the donut shop. The locksmith had installed a new lock on the door and supplied new sets of keys to the staff. Maggie and Ruby worked together to close up the food truck and resumed cleaning the big kitchen. A peek at the video camera footage from the security cameras outside the donut shop revealed very little, aside from a dark figure hanging out around the back door. The video was too blurry to determine the gender of the intruder.

"Might be time to get better quality cameras," Ruby said.

"That or we're going to need to park the food truck in the alley behind the donut shop every night when we close up for the day," Maggie suggested.

Brett shook his head. "I wouldn't recommend that." He had come back a short time after his daughter left and chosen to remain behind for a little while after the rest of the police had finished up inside the donut shop.

"Why not?" Maggie asked. "We could prevent anyone from coming in the back door."

"And block the alley from any emergency vehicles that might need to get through, which could affect the outcome of your insurance if there is a fire," he said.

"A fire! That's the last thing I want to think about." Maggie groaned and glared at Brett for putting the idea in her head.

"Not to mention the fact that all they have to do is go around to the front door and break the glass," Ruby added.

Every which way she turned, someone was shooting down her idea. Maggie knew they were right, but she wasn't exactly thinking clearly and was only trying to come up with some sort of solution. "I guess that's not much of an option. What are the chances we'll get hit again?"

Brett shook his head. "Not huge," he said. "It's very uncommon for a business to be hit twice in a short amount of time, statistically speaking. Sort of like lightning striking twice in the same place."

"So, you don't think we have much to worry about?" Ruby asked.

Brett rose to leave. "I don't think you need to post an armed guard, and as the police chief I would frown on that anyway, but I think you should invest in some better cameras," he said. "Heck, even those doorbell cameras would take better videos."

After he left, Maggie busied herself thoroughly cleaning the floors in the shop. She'd wanted to talk to him about his daughter. She'd wanted to tell him that sometimes kids had what they considered great ideas and trying to stop them or convince them otherwise would only serve to cause more problems, but it was clear to see that he had no desire to talk about it. He was as kind as ever, but she could tell by his clenched jaw and rigid mannerisms that he wasn't his normal self. He'd come to her when he was ready.

Ruby hung around and gave every surface in the kitchen a good sanitizing clean. Afterward, they worked together on the cooler.

"I think it's time we change our hiding place for petty cash," Ruby said as she rearranged some of the boxes in front of her.

Maggie agreed. "I think I'll start taking it home with me every day."

"Are you sure that's a good idea?"

"No one will ever suspect it," she said. "I'll just start putting the cash bag in my bag when I leave. I think I'm going to pick up one of those fireproof boxes for my house anyway."

"That's not a bad idea." Ruby turned to her. "I think we might need to consider not keeping cash around at all. Other than what's in the register, I mean. We could leave ourselves a receipt and take cash from there if we really need something."

Maggie paused, holding a covered bowl of edible brownie batter in her hands. "I hate this. I hate that we can't leave cash around. I hate that someone thought breaking into our shop was a good idea. I hate that whoever it was knew where we keep our things. What do you think that means?"

Ruby sighed and looked Maggie in the eyes. "If you're asking me if I think one of our employees could have stolen from us, the answer is no. And I'm not just saying that because that would also mean they would have robbed several other places. Myra and Orson simply wouldn't do anything like that, and you know it. On the other hand, your aunt Marjorie also kept her petty cash in the cooler, and she had several people in and out of here working over the years back when she owned the place. She liked to hire high school or college kids or people who were down on their luck. I can think of at least twice when she hired someone off the street who looked hungry and like they could use a few bucks. She'd have them work for a couple hours a day washing dishes or working on inventory."

"You mean random people that she didn't vet and get an application from? No background checks or anything?"

"Maggie, please remind me when you got a background check on me, Myra, or Orson…"

Ruby didn't need to finish her thought before Maggie interrupted, "I get it and you're right. But all I'm saying is that just means even more people could have thought to look here for money. What if those random people worked at all of these local businesses and knew where to look for what they wanted?"

"That feels like an awful lot of what ifs," Ruby said. "Do you really want to spend all your time wondering who it was, or should we maybe focus on making sure we are more protected from things like this happening again in the future?"

"Both," Maggie admitted. "I want to know why someone would do that to us."

"That's the thing. I'm not so sure someone did this to us specifically. You know it happened to other businesses and this might not be a direct hit on the donut shop or anyone in it." Ruby stepped back from her workspace and checked to make sure everything was in order.

"Yeah," Maggie said simply and left it at that. They worked in a comfortable silence until the cooler was reorganized and the prep work was finished for the following morning.

"I'm going to get out of here," Ruby said. "Want to come over later?"

Maggie let out a tired sigh that surprised even herself. "I need to go to the hardware store to check out some cameras and then I think I should just go home and spend some time with Bradley and Wyatt before I fall into bed for the night."

"I hear ya. Call me if you need anything." Ruby gave her a quick hug and together they locked up the shop and headed out to their vehicles.

CHAPTER FOUR

Ruby headed back to the farm, and Maggie headed to the hardware store. At first, she wandered the aisles mindlessly. Her brain needed a break from thinking after the events of the day.

"Hello again," a voice called out to her when she reached the end of the pet aisle.

Maggie looked up into the face of the young woman who had appeared at the food truck earlier in the day. While a conversation with her might not require thinking, she wasn't looking forward to whatever situation was about to occur. She had no idea if Layla knew who she was or if Brett had said anything to her about their relationship.

"Hello," she greeted the younger woman. "It's Layla, right?"

The girl nodded and smiled brightly. Maggie saw the clear resemblance to her father then. "You look like your dad when you smile."

A shadow crossed the girl's pretty face. "My dad would say that is the only way I resemble him. He has a hard time accepting anything I do."

"That's the way it is for parents and children," Maggie said, preparing herself for a heavy conversation she didn't want to have. The last thing she wanted to do was step between Brett and his daughter. "But you should know it generally means that the parent sees a great deal of potential in the child."

"Do you have kids?" Layla asked her.

Maggie nodded her head and grinned. "My son is on leave from the Navy at the moment. He is staying at my house with his newborn son."

"Wow," Layla said. "I didn't think you were old enough to be a grandma."

Maggie chuckled. "I'm the same age as your dad. We went to high school together."

"Oh, I am so sorry," Layla said. "That sounded so wrong. He told me about you…"

Before Layla could finish, a tall, older woman with the same chestnut brown hair color walked up next to her. "What are you sorry for?" the woman asked. She eyed Maggie sharply.

"Maggie, this is my mother, Corinne," Layla said. "Mom, I accidentally spoke out of turn about Maggie's age."

"Oh, is that all?" Corinne waved her hand in the air. "Who cares about that?"

"Mom," Layla said under her breath.

Corinne ignored her daughter. "And how are the two of you so acquainted?"

"Oh, the donut shop lady!" Layla's companion Tommy joined them. "Good to see you again."

"Hello, Tommy," Maggie said. She was suddenly even more weary of the conversation.

"Ahhh, the donut lady." Corinne smirked. "You work at the local donut shop?"

"I own Dogwood Donuts, yes," Maggie said evenly. She refused to let her fatigue or any other emotion show.

"Oh, I thought maybe you just ran the food truck," Tommy said.

Maggie shook her head. "We operated out of the food truck yesterday after a burglary, but that's rather new for us. It's the main shop that's our focus."

"That's why Dad was there," Layla explained to both her boyfriend and her mother. "I think it's pretty neat that you could run the food truck while your business was shut down for the day. I've always admired people who can come up with a quick fix when something goes wrong."

Maggie smiled despite her frustration with the conversation. "Thanks," she said. "I'm glad, too. The food truck has been a blessing for us."

"Who has a food truck?" A fourth person joined the group. He rested his arm around Corinne's shoulders.

"She does," Tommy pointed. "She owns the donut shop."

"Oh." The man frowned. "You were robbed, weren't you?"

Maggie nodded, wishing these people weren't visiting the hardware store as a family. She gripped the handle of her cart impatiently. "That's actually why I'm here," she said. "I need to upgrade some security measures."

"You need to do more than that," the man said. "Who is your insurance agent and what is he doing about it?"

Layla cleared her throat. "Steven, I think Maggie has other things to do besides hear an insurance pitch from you."

"Watch it, young lady." Corinne's eyes flashed. "Steven is only trying to help."

She pulled her cart away and noticed the look on

Brett's daughter's face. If nothing else, she had to give the girl credit for being so polite. Maggie wished she'd gotten to hear the rest of what Layla was going to say earlier. She selfishly wanted to know if Brett had told her about them or not. Either he had and that's why Layla was being nice or maybe Layla was just all around a nicer person than her mother was.

"It was great to meet all of you, but I really do need to get going," she said.

"Wait, before you go," Steven said. He pulled a card out of his wallet and handed it over. "Call me and I'll come by later and assess your security needs. I also want to look over the policies on both your business and that food truck you have."

Maggie turned the card over in her hand. "I will speak with my business partner and let you know," she said and took a couple of steps away from the group.

"We'll just stop by ourselves." Corinne wound her arm through Steven's, much as Layla had done through Tommy's earlier. "I haven't eaten a donut in so many years. I've almost forgotten what they taste like."

Maggie excused herself and headed for the doorbell cameras. She hurried to make her selections and went right to the registers. When she approached the cashier, she almost turned away. Layla and her family were gathered around the register next to her.

"Let's just go," Layla was saying to her mother. Maggie tried not to listen. She didn't want to know what family drama brewed around them. She angled her cart toward the other register.

"Who is this guy?" Maggie heard Steven ask.

"Just somebody I knew in high school," Layla replied. Despite her growing curiosity, Maggie forced herself to keep her eyes down. She wanted to look, but she didn't want any more information whirling around in her brain at the moment.

"He's hardly just someone you knew," Corinne said. "They dated seriously through her senior year. He got down on one knee at her senior prom."

"Mom," Layla said. Her voice rose.

Maggie looked up into the reddened face of another young man. He was dressed in khaki pants and a pullover shirt sporting the hardware store logo. She glanced at his name tag. "Drew," she said aloud.

"Yes," Drew said.

Maggie almost covered her mouth with her hand, but she decided to run with it. "Are you a cashier?"

Drew smiled. His face muscles seemed to relax, though he glanced one more time toward Layla and her family. His face was friendly and pleasant, though

Maggie could see how he might feel intimidated by the tall, good-looking, and athletic Tommy. Drew was average but built solidly. Maggie imagined a hardworking farmer when she looked at him. "Yes, ma'am," he said. "I can help you right here."

Maggie followed him to the open line and placed her items on the belt. "Thank you," she told him. As he scanned her items, his eyes ventured over her head toward Layla.

"Is everything okay?" Maggie asked him.

"Um, yeah," Drew said. "Sorry. I'm a bit distracted."

"Yeah, I get it," Maggie said. "Some people can be distracting."

"I'm so sorry, ma'am," Drew said. "You deserve better than a cashier who can't focus. I see you have purchased security cameras. If you'd like, we can help set up installation services for you. Of course, there is no obligation, but there is a trick to getting these doorbell cameras synced up with your cell phone. It's quite easy if you know what you are doing, but if not or if you'd rather have some help, we can absolutely take care of that for you."

The sudden change in the young man's demeanor took her off guard. She was unsure if his offer to help was sincere or just a coverup for his bad manners. "I think I'll check with my son first to see if he can do it," she said.

"For sure, yeah. Well, let us know if we can help," Drew said with a smile. "Now, would you like help out to your car?"

Maggie denied any help and hurried out of the hardware store to her car, hoping to avoid any more conversations with the people inside.

"Long day?" Bradley asked when she made it home at last.

Maggie nodded. She set her bags on the table and moved to the kitchen to wash her hands. "I just bought the hardware store out of doorbell cameras for the donut shop," she said. "I was hoping you might be able to set them up for me sometime."

"I can sure try," he said as he handed his son over to Maggie's outstretched arms. "He's cranky. I'm not sure what's up with him this evening."

"Hello, Wyatt," Maggie cooed at her grandson. "Why aren't you giving your daddy a break?"

"Speaking of a break," Bradley said. "Can you keep an eye on him while I take a shower?"

Maggie nodded. "Take a shower and then a nap," she said. "Wyatt and I can hang out while I make something for dinner and call Aunt Ruby."

Bradley shook his head. "I feel like I can't do

anything but hold him all day," he said. "How do you make dinner and handle business matters at the same time?"

Maggie shrugged her shoulders and chuckled. "It's called just learning to do what you have to do, son."

She looked at Wyatt as Bradley went off to shower and nap. No matter how tired Maggie was, she did what she had to do. She was a mother first and her son needed her. Soon, he'd learn the way things went with a new baby, but for now, she could stay up for a few more hours to make sure the people she loved the most in life were taken care of.

CHAPTER FIVE

The next morning, Maggie gathered her things quietly. For once, Wyatt had slept for longer than just a couple of hours in a row. She had turned her phone on silent the night before as to not wake anyone up. She picked up her bags from the kitchen table and headed out to the car.

When she reached the car, Maggie turned her phone on. She drove the short distance to work and was surprised not to see Ruby's truck parked out back. Maggie and Ruby agreed to arrive at work at the same time after what had happened.

Maggie's phone began chirping when she put her car in park. She picked it up out of her bag and began reading through the messages. "Hold on before you head for work," Ruby had texted. "The outdoor spigot sprung a leak in the middle of the night. I'm running late."

Maggie sighed. She knew Ruby would tell her to wait before getting out of her car and going into the donut shop. But the door was still firmly secured from what she could see. She turned her lights back on and drove around to the parking lot. She stopped just outside of the front door to examine the glass. Everything appeared to be locked up tight.

Lightning rarely struck twice, right?

Maggie decided to trust in the small likelihood that the donut shop would be hit a second time in one week. She gathered her bag and readied the keys for a quick entrance. She had her phone in her hand and was ready in case she needed to make a quick phone call.

The new lock on the back door was stiff when she pushed in her key, but it opened at last, and she headed straight for the light switch. She decided to take a quick pass through every part of the building before she relaxed. In the back, she looked through the storeroom, the cooler, and the office. She opened the door to the employee restroom and then made her way back through the kitchen.

The dining room was well-lit and empty. Still, Maggie looked under every table and chair. She opened the door to the ladies' room and checked the stalls, then did the same thing in the men's room. Satisfied that there was no danger, Maggie headed back to the kitchen. She texted Ruby on her way through the swinging door.

"All is well," she wrote. "I checked every square inch of the place. Getting ready to turn everything on and get the day started." She set her phone on the baker's table and headed for the donut machines. She switched on the deep fryer next and headed for the cooler.

Maggie had spent weeks researching new recipes. Last year, it was Orson who blew everyone's socks off with his apple-themed ideas. And this year, Maggie was determined to bring new flavors to the menu. Pears would be her focus. She added a crumb-topped pear cider donut and scone to the menu and planned to give away samples of a spiced pear cider over the next few days.

She planned to start the automatic donut machines as soon as the oil was hot enough. At the baker's table, she would begin work on her new pear-themed offerings. She planned to chop several pears for the batter and then add several more to the food processor to prepare a puree for the cider. The pears were situated on the top shelf of the cooler. Maggie filled both arms with the containers of pears and pushed against the cooler door with her elbow.

The cooler door gave way. Maggie looked down to balance the load in her arms. She took two steps into the kitchen and let the door close behind her. When the door closed, the hair on the back of her neck stood on end. She felt the presence of another person behind her. She took another step forward but was stopped when the arm of the unseen person circled around her neck.

"Don't move." The arm tightened, and she felt something cold pressed against her skin.

"What do you want?" she asked.

"Shut up," the voice responded. Maggie made note of the thick rasp of the voice. It was almost one hundred percent male, and she was sure disguised. The arm around her neck seemed to pull upward, and she was sure that the assailant was a great deal taller than she was.

"I don't have anything here but a few hundred dollars in petty cash," she said. Her voice, to her surprise, remained calm.

"I know what you have here," he said. "Move." He pulled on her, dragging her toward the office.

Maggie lost her grip on the containers in her arms. Pears and bowls crashed to the floor and scattered around her feet. "I'm just trying to get things ready to open. Tell me what you want so I can help you get it, and I can get on with my day."

"I said, shut up!" Maggie looked down as far as she could. Light from overhead glinted off of the steel blade.

"Okay, okay," Maggie said. A wave of fear passed through her. She wondered for the first time if he was there to hurt her, or worse.

When they reached the office, Maggie heard the door open behind her. The intruder turned her around and shoved her inside. She launched forward and fell to the floor, landing hard on her knees and palms.

"Ouch!" she shouted.

The door slammed behind her. "Don't you dare come back out here," the raspy voice shouted through the door.

Maggie crawled to the other side of the small office. She pushed her body under the small desk and pulled the office chair in front of her. Her shoulders began to tremble. She raised her hands and slowly reached for the desk phone.

Likely, the intruder hadn't counted on a landline in the office, she thought.

She picked up the receiver and held it to her ear

and waited for the dial tone. Slowly she pecked out Ruby's cell phone number.

"Ruby," she whispered into the phone. "Don't come to the shop. Someone is here. Don't come. Call the police."

"Where are you?" Ruby asked.

"Office," Maggie whispered. "He's got a knife."

"Are you hurt?" Ruby asked. Maggie heard the deep roar of the truck's engine through the phone.

"I don't think so. But seriously, Ruby. Call Brett. But don't come."

"I'm headed to town now," Ruby said. "Stay on the line with me and I'll stop at the police station to tell them. I'm almost there."

Maggie heard something scoot across the floor outside the office door. "He's still here. I have to go." She could hear Ruby's protests when she hung up the phone.

As soon as she set the phone back up on the desk the door flew open again. Maggie made out the figure in the door. "Who are you talking to?" the intruder demanded.

"I uhh… I was saying a prayer," Maggie answered. "I'm a little bit scared."

"Just stay put and you won't get hurt," he said gruffly and slammed the door again.

CHAPTER SIX

"Tell me everything you can remember about him," Brett said. Maggie sat across from him at the donut shop. Once again, he had come into work early to respond to the call.

"He was taller than me, by quite a bit," she said. "His voice was gruff, and I think he was trying to disguise it. He was strong, too." She brushed her fingers over the broken skin on her neck.

"Do you have any idea what he was doing?" Brett asked her.

Maggie shook her head. As soon as the police arrived and removed her from the office, she had instructed them to check for the petty cash bag which was still hidden in her purse. Nothing had been touched, including the secondhand iPad she had brought from home to use as a register.

"I just don't get it," Maggie said. "I could hear him dragging things all over the kitchen. I stayed put because I thought he had barricaded me in the office."

Brett nodded his head. "We could see the scuff marks on the floor. And I know the layout of the kitchen well enough myself to know he moved plenty of things around. What he was looking for, we can't be sure."

"Now what?" Maggie asked. "I don't want to shut down for another full day."

Brett stood and looked at the clock over the counter. "We have a couple of hours to process the scene," he said. "But I think I would fire up the food truck just in case. In the meantime, you should go home and get some rest. Let Ruby handle things for today."

"I'm not going to do that," she said. "Ruby is wonderful to help out as much as she does, but this is the business my aunt left to me, and I am just not going to let this get me down. I know there are other times and places where I have to sit on the sidelines, but not today."

"Maggie." Brett reached across the table and laid his hand on her arm. "Listen to me, you need to take it easy. You have been through something traumatic, and you might end up with a traumatic response to it."

She didn't move her arm for a long moment. After a few deep breaths, Maggie locked eyes with Brett. "I appreciate your concern, and I know you are worried about me, but I am going to open like normal and work through any response," she said. "If I go home, Bradley and Wyatt will need me, and I will get lost in helping them. But if I'm here, there are others around that will check up on me and make me feel cared for, and I think I need that today."

Brett nodded, apparently satisfied by her explanation. "Well, we will do our very best to get out of the way so you can open like normal," he said.

Afterward, Maggie grabbed the keys to the food truck from the office and headed out to fire up the deep fryer and the mini donut machine. Ruby was still out back in the alley behind the donut shop helping another officer look over the back door. Maggie found her and nodded toward the front parking lot.

"I'm going to get things ready in the truck," she announced. "Come and find me when you're finished here." Maggie didn't wait for a reply. Instead, she headed straight for the front parking lot and opened the back of the food truck.

Once inside, Maggie turned on everything she

needed to and started a pot of coffee in one of the industrial pots. She prepared the first batch of batter for the donut machine, and then poured herself a cup of coffee and sat down at the small bistro set.

When the donut machine began to drop the batter into the hot oil Maggie finished off her cup of coffee and gazed out over the parking lot. She could see into the front windows where Ruby was standing by the front counter speaking with Brett and another officer.

"Any chance of opening up like normal?" Maggie texted Ruby. She watched as Ruby pulled her phone out of her pocket and glanced out the window in her direction.

"Let's plan to open an hour late," Ruby typed back. "Brett said they will finish up by six-thirty."

"I'll keep preparations going out here for the time being and make the announcement on social media," Maggie typed back.

By eight, the donut shop buzzed with activity like normal. Myra decided to run the food truck in the parking lot offering mini donuts for walk-up customers. Inside the big kitchen, Maggie stuck to working at the baker's table while Ruby and Orson ran the front.

"How are things going back here?" Orson ventured back to ask her once every half-hour.

"I'm really okay, Orson," Maggie said on his fifth or sixth trip back. "It was a bad ordeal, but I am trying to work past it. Really."

"There are some things in life you can't just work past," Orson said. "I think you need to talk to somebody about this." He then turned on his heel and headed back out of the kitchen.

Maggie ignored his words and punched her fist into the ball of dough on the table in front of her instead. She worked for the next hour on three batches of cinnamon rolls and set them on the racks to rise.

When the cinnamon rolls were ready to bake, Maggie ventured to the front for a refill on her coffee. "How are things going?" Ruby whispered when she got close.

"Alright." Maggie forced a smile. "I have the cinnamon rolls baking and the pear scones are up next."

"How about a short break?" Ruby suggested. "Our booth is empty. I could use a cup of something caffeinated myself."

Maggie hesitated. "Are you sure this isn't another attempt to check on me and make sure I'm alright?" she asked. She'd said earlier that she wanted to feel cared for, but she had to admit that she didn't love everyone doting on her. She'd much rather have had the time to talk to Brett about his daughter or Orson about Gretchen, but she knew everyone was more worried about her than themselves right now and she was thankful for that, even if it made her feel a little bit awkward.

"Only partially." Ruby winked. "I'm really dead on my feet."

"Let me check on things in the back," Maggie said.

"I've got it." Orson slid off of the barstool he was seated on and headed for the swinging door. "It's been pretty quiet in here for a little while. I think Myra is handling things outside just fine."

Maggie gazed at their normal booth and sighed. The weight of the day was beginning to settle on her shoulders, and it was just the middle of the morning. "You twisted my arm." She smiled, and then suddenly frowned when she thought of the manhandling she had endured a few hours before. "That came out wrong."

"We need something a little stronger than coffee, I think," Ruby joked. She led Maggie to the booth and took the seat across from her. "Tell me how you're doing."

Maggie smiled and shrugged half-heartedly. "I am functioning," she said.

"Do you think it would be better if you were at home?"

Maggie shook her head. "No, to be honest. This is better. Busy is better," she said. "At home, I might help out holding Wyatt while Bradley gets some rest, but that means a lot more quiet moments where my mind can twist and turn like crazy. Someone broke in here for the second time in a matter of a few days."

"And held you at knifepoint," Ruby said gently.

"And held me at knifepoint, yes," she said. "The last thing I want to do is go home and stew in my own thoughts in the quiet."

Orson set two mugs of coffee between them. He said nothing but gave Maggie a pat on the shoulder before he turned to go back to the counter.

"I swear he is growing more and more paternal by the day."

Maggie picked up her mug and smiled slightly. "You won't find me complaining."

"Me either," Ruby said. "Speaking of fathers, what's going on with Brett and his daughter?"

"I don't know, other than there's a whole lot of drama around that whole situation," Maggie said. "Did I tell you about running into them in the hardware store?"

"No." Ruby leaned in, ready for the best bit of gossip.

Before Maggie launched into the tale, she fought the urge to reach out and clasp her best friend's hands in her own. Thank goodness for the distraction, she thought.

"I saw the whole clan, at least, Layla and her new boyfriend, her mom, Corinne, and her boyfriend, Steven, and even one of Layla's old high school boyfriends," she said. "They held me in one place forever asking me questions."

"Sounds like a nightmare." Ruby laughed.

"It really was," Maggie said. "First, it's Brett's ex-wife. Second, her boyfriend, Steven, nearly interrogated me about my insurance policies on both the donut shop and the food truck. He even gave me his business card."

"Oh, one of those types." Ruby rolled her eyes. For a moment, Maggie wondered how much of her reaction was genuine and how much was for her benefit, to provide more distraction from the attack earlier in the morning. Almost as soon as she composed the thought, she decided she didn't care one way or the other.

"Exactly. I thought I would never get out of there.

I told him that I am perfectly content with the coverage I have," Maggie said.

"Maybe he's trying to infiltrate an already saturated market." Ruby picked up her mug once more and gazed over Maggie's head. The bells on the front door chimed. Maggie decided to save herself the effort of turning around to look and see who had come in.

"Just tell me if we need to cut our break short," Maggie said. "Otherwise, I don't care who that is."

"Tell me something," Ruby said. Her eyes darted between Maggie's face and the view behind her. "This Steven guy, was he tall, dark-headed, built like a linebacker for the Chiefs?"

"Yeah," Maggie said timidly. "Why?"

"Because I think he just walked in here with the entire crew," Ruby said. She lowered her mouth to her coffee cup. "And they are headed this way."

CHAPTER SEVEN

"Maggie?"

Maggie turned around to see a smiling Corinne standing over her. "Hello, again," she said.

Corinne stood just a few feet from the booth and pressed her hands to her chest. "Honey, I was so shocked to hear about what happened to you this morning," she said. "Are you alright?"

Maggie glanced at Ruby before she answered. "Yes, I'm okay," she said. "This is my best friend and business partner, Ruby Cobb."

Ruby raised her fingers in a wave, but Corinne paid no attention. "I have to say that I'm surprised to see you here," she continued. "I could almost have my ex-husband horsewhipped for allowing you to remain open and working after what you've been through."

"Mom," Layla interrupted. "I'm sure it isn't Dad's fault."

"Nor would it be his decision," Steven interjected. "I hope you will reconsider my offer to come and have a look at your security needs around here now, Maggie."

"I thought you sold insurance," Ruby said.

"I do," Steven said, reaching into his pocket and producing another business card. "But a good agent will write the policy based on his client's wishes. A great agent will walk around in his client's shoes and tell them what their needs are."

Maggie cringed slightly and made up her mind that Steven Mendoza would never insure anything she owned, even if he was the last agent on the planet. "I need to set up the cameras I bought at the hardware store yesterday," Maggie said.

"Oh, I figured old Drew would have taken care of that for you," Tommy said. He pulled Layla closer to him.

"The young man at the hardware store?" Ruby asked.

"Yeah, he fancies himself some sort of security expert," Corinne said with a smirk.

"He never said a word to me about that," Maggie said. "He just offered to help me if I needed it."

"Drew Lee is trying to start his own security systems installation business," Ruby explained to Maggie. "It's something the owner of the hardware store actually encourages. He talked to me not that long ago to see if I needed any security systems installed at the farm. The hardware store would get the business from the security systems and Drew would do the installations, so it'd be a win-win for everyone."

"Oh," Maggie said. She nodded her head in approval. If Drew's boss encouraged him to start his own business, then maybe hiring him wasn't such a bad idea after all. It was likely that Bradley could set everything up for her, but he had his hands full with Wyatt and it was never a bad idea to work closely with other local businesses.

"It's nothing but a joke," Tommy scoffed. "That's what it is."

"Drew still carries a torch for our Layla here," Corinne added. "They dated in high school."

"Ah, okay," Maggie said. She fought the temptation to ask why any of this was relevant to her. "I originally planned to have my son install the doorbell cameras, but I may look into Drew further." She hadn't yet decided what to do but being contrary felt like the right thing to do. These people were driving her crazy.

"Is your son some kind of expert?" Steven asked. "Not that it matters. Anyone is better than Drew." Maggie didn't appreciate his tone of voice.

"Her son is on leave from the United States Navy and worthy of respect," Orson's voice boomed behind them. "Now, why don't you folks follow me to the front counter, and I can take your order?"

"Remind me to hug that man's neck when those awful people leave," Maggie muttered to Ruby when they headed back to the kitchen.

"I think he's going to enjoy the dinner I make for him tonight," Ruby said. "Are you up for a bonfire this evening?"

"You better believe it." Maggie smiled. "I'm sure Bradley would be, too."

"Might be the last one before he and Wyatt head to Oklahoma, right?"

"Yeah." Maggie sighed. "I'm torn between utter despair and relief to see them go."

"I don't think you're a bad person either way," Ruby said. "Why don't you text Bradley and I'll speak to Myra and Orson?"

"Sounds good to me," Maggie said. "What about Brooks?"

"Brooks and Brett will also be invited," Ruby said. "I'm sure Myra will let him know and you can fill Brett in. I think it's safe to say we all need a little break from regular life right now and what better way than a bonfire at my house?"

"You aren't wrong," Maggie agreed. "I'm definitely looking forward to it."

"You know, I think we ought to close down for the day tomorrow," Ruby said out of nowhere.

"Close down? Why?" Maggie pulled a batch of cinnamon rolls out of the oven. "We've already lost some time this week with the first break-in."

"That's exactly why we should shut down." Ruby picked up a towel and tossed it in the linen hamper a few feet from the storeroom door. "We've suffered two break-ins in the space of a few days. You have those doorbell cameras that we need to install. I say let's make the announcement online and close our doors long enough to install the cameras and any other security measures we see fit."

"Should we call Mr. Mendoza to supervise?" Maggie grinned and set the second pan of cinnamon rolls on the glazer.

"While I appreciate your feistiness, I think we

might find someone far more qualified than that," Ruby said. "I'm going to bring it up to Brett and Brooks tonight. Maybe we'll have them drop by as well."

"I actually think I want to hire Drew Lee to install them," Maggie said.

"Good idea. Somehow, I want to give that young man all the business we can. If he's caught up with that group of misfits in any way, I can't help but feel bad for him. Brett's daughter seems like the only normal one of the bunch."

"That's pretty much how I feel, too." Maggie readied the first tray of cinnamon rolls for the glazer while Ruby packed boxed lunches on an empty tray to set in the large stainless steel refrigerator behind the front counter.

They worked in the back together for the rest of the day and both women couldn't have been more thankful to see the Open sign flipped to Closed. They definitely needed a break.

CHAPTER EIGHT

When she drove down the rural gravel road to Ruby's farm, Maggie saw some familiar cars already parked in the driveway. Myra's car was parked behind Orson's, and Maggie pulled hers to the side of both. She parked and got out with two grocery bags full of salad fixings.

"Ruby?" she called her friend's name when she walked through the back door.

"In here," Ruby said. Maggie walked through the kitchen and set her bags down on the butcher block island then followed Ruby's voice through the house to the dining room. Orson was seated at the head of the table.

"Is everything alright?" Maggie asked, suddenly worried about what was going on.

"Yeah," Myra said. She was seated on Orson's right. "We're just talking."

Maggie noted the painful look on Orson's face. "You don't look alright," she said. "What's going on?"

As much as her grumpy employee and friend liked to make her cringe with his caustic comments, she was quite aware that something might be going on with him and Gretchen. "Are you and Gretchen okay?"

"What do you mean are we okay? Why wouldn't we be okay? What have you heard?" Orson blurted. He looked around the room waiting for an answer from someone.

"It's just that Myra said you came home early from a date with Gretchen and I..." Maggie couldn't get the words out without an interruption.

"Oh." He dismissed her worry with a wave. "We're just fine. She was caught up with Brett's daughter and that boyfriend of hers. I have enough on my plate and too much information in my head about all you people. I certainly didn't need to know the goings on about the chief's daughter or better yet, my boss's boyfriend's daughter. I'm not sure which sounds worse, but whatever it is, I pick that.

Maggie grinned. "Well, then I guess you're just fine and I'm worried about nothing."

"I wouldn't go that far," Myra chimed in.

"Yeah, Orson here is having a hard time with what took place yesterday," Ruby said, almost whispering.

"Are you talking about the attack in the donut shop?" Maggie asked.

Orson nodded. "I should have protected you," he said softly.

"You should have protected me?" Maggie took a seat at the table next to Myra. She reached out and took the man's hand in her own. "Orson, that isn't your responsibility."

"Why not?" Orson asked, barely raising his voice. "Your son is around, but he has a newborn to care for. You have Brooks to look out for you," he said to Myra.. "But you two, I'm old fashioned but I see it as my responsibility to watch over you girls. Maggie, I know you've got Brett but he's busy protecting the entire town so we can't rely on him. It's my job and I let you down."

Ruby grinned slightly, and Maggie caught her amusement at his reference to the two of them, one in her forties and the other in her fifties, as "girls."

"But you do protect us," Maggie said. "No one could have known that an intruder was in the donut shop, lying in wait. I looked around the entire building and saw no one. There's simply no way anyone could have known. We don't even know how they got in there to begin with."

"And Orson, even if our fathers were still alive or if we were married, I don't think any man would have known that Maggie was going to be attacked," Ruby said. "And you did a pretty good job protecting us earlier today when those people wouldn't leave us alone."

Orson nodded half-heartedly. "I just wish I could be more effective," he said.

"You do more than enough to help everyone at the donut shop. We wouldn't want to do any of this without you, right girls?" Ruby winked.

"She's right, you know," Myra said, giving Orson a nudge.

"Yeah, yeah. Whatever you all say. I can't believe you were worried about my love life." He huffed.

"Anyway," Maggie said, rising from the table. "I need some help preparing this epic salad in the other room."

"On it," Myra said.

"In the meantime, I need you to accompany me outdoors," Ruby said to Orson.

"What for?" he asked.

"To watch the bonfire, and to welcome everyone

when they drive up," she said.

"You're just trying to get me out of the house," Orson muttered. Maggie smiled at his full return to his normal grumpy self.

"Maybe, but at least you can sit outside in the evening air with a drink in your hand while the rest of us work to prepare your dinner," Myra said. "Come on, Orson. I keep telling you that this old man gig is better than you think it is."

CHAPTER NINE

Myra joined Maggie in the kitchen where they worked together to prepare the large garden salad. "Any idea what the main course is going to be?" Maggie asked.

"I have heard talk of filets, and grilled Hasselback potatoes, but I know that's just part of the feast she has planned," Myra said.

Maggie hefted the large, covered bowl through the back door and out to the outdoor kitchen where Ruby had prepared a place for it to stay cold until dinner was served. Already, Maggie could see the orange flames glowing against the barns in the twilight.

"When will the guys arrive?" she asked Ruby, who was already busy at the grill.

"Bradley got here just a bit ago with Wyatt. I see he got himself a new car," Ruby said approvingly.

"Yeah, he bought a used car for his drive to Oklahoma. He was so proud of the safety rating." She was secretly delighted in his sudden awareness of safety matters and other new parent discoveries.

"Good for him," Ruby said over her shoulder. "Orson has them both entertained for now, but I think Brooks and Brett are both running late. Brett said the two of them would be here by seven."

"Someone is coming now," Myra said, gazing down the gravel road at the cloud of dust rising in the distance.

"And they're coming in hot and fast," Maggie said. "Slow down idiot!"

"Uh-oh." Myra laughed "I think you just called your boyfriend an idiot."

"Oops." Maggie shrugged. "But still, he is going a little faster than necessary."

"There are two cars," Myra said. She walked closer to the driveway. "I see two cars coming. It's the chief and Brooks right behind him."

Ruby turned from the grill when Brett pulled to a stop in her driveway. "Where is everyone?" he asked.

"We're all here." Myra waved at him. Maggie followed her and walked out closer to the grill.

"Orson, Bradley and the baby are just over there." She pointed.

Brooks pulled up behind him and got out of the car as well. "Have you told them yet?" he asked the chief.

"Told us what?" Maggie asked. She waved Orson and Bradley over.

"Everyone, let's sit down," Brett suggested. "Can you take a break for a second, Ruby?"

"Yeah, give me a minute," she said and shut the flame off under the steaks. She placed the filets on a platter and then set them under another grill hood to keep warm. When she was finished, Ruby took a seat and they waited in silence while Bradley made sure Wyatt was settled.

"Are you guys going to let us in on what is going on?" Orson asked, much too impatient to wait.

"We just left a crime scene behind the hardware store," Brett announced.

Myra threw her hands in the air. "Let me guess, another robbery," she said.

"Doesn't sound like a robbery to me." Maggie frowned. "Not if it was behind the hardware store."

"It wasn't another robbery," Brett continued. "A body was found in a car parked just outside the back door, in broad daylight."

"Who?" Ruby asked.

Brooks hung his head. "Drew Lee, the young man who worked there," he said.

"Oh, gosh." Maggie gasped. She stood up to take Wyatt from Bradley. The infant seemed to sense the somber change in mood surrounding him. "We were just talking about hiring him to install doorbell cameras at the donut shop." She swayed side to side with Wyatt in her arms.

"There's more," Brooks said.

Brett nodded soberly. "He was found in his vehicle with a bag of incriminating evidence on the seat next to him."

"What incriminating evidence?" Ruby asked.

"A black ski mask, black leather gloves, a lock pick kit, as well as a sharp hunting knife," Brett said with a sigh. "It looks like we might have found our burglar."

Maggie felt her entire body clench. The sweet kid who she was going to hire was the one who broke into her shop and held a knife to her neck. How much more wrong about someone could she be?

"I don't believe that!" Orson declared. "It doesn't make sense."

"What do you mean?" Brett asked. "Why doesn't this make sense to you?"

Orson raised his chin and nodded toward town. "You say he was found dead?" he asked. "Was he murdered? Was it natural causes? Did he maybe end his own life?"

"We really can't say at this point in the investigation," Brooks admitted.

"But there is an investigation," Orson said. "Which tells me that it wasn't a clear-cut case of him doing himself in."

"Okay, but what's your point?" Brett asked.

"If this young man was going around burglarizing local businesses and holding knives to the throats of innocent women, who would know enough to kill him?" Orson asked. "Wouldn't he be more likely to be the dangerous one?"

"And why would he commit suicide if there was absolutely no pressure on him from an investigation closing in on him?" Bradley asked.

"All good points," Brett agreed. "But it's too early to know much of anything."

"He's being set up." Maggie shifted a now-sleeping baby to her shoulder and gently patted his back.

"How do you know that?" Brett asked her. "If you know something, Maggie, please let us in on it." He kept his voice down, but the urgency in his tone was clear.

"Because," Maggie said. "I stood face to face with him just a day ago or so. And he was not tall enough to be the guy who attacked me. I'm still not convinced that it wasn't an ex-employee from the donut shop before I took over."

"Wait, what?" Brett asked, exchanging a look with Brooks. "What do you mean an ex-employee? And why is this the first I'm hearing about it?"

"Whoever broke in knew where we kept our money and Ruby said my Aunt Marjorie used to do the same thing. What if it was someone who used to work for her?" Maggie asked.

"Okay, but what about all the other businesses?" Brooks challenged. "I think your point is valid, but what are the chances that one person worked for all of those places?"

"Fine." Maggie nodded. "Then what if we were all wrong and maybe Drew's boss wasn't all that happy and encouraging about him starting his own business installing security cameras? Maybe he found out about what Drew was doing and something escalated, and he killed him?"

"He is a tall man." Ruby crossed her arms as though she was satisfied with her realization.

"Another decent point," Brett agreed. "But you go from one extreme to the next. Are you saying he was framed by his boss or that he's the one who broke in to all these businesses and somehow got himself killed because of it?"

Maggie didn't know what she was saying. She had no more of an idea what happened than anyone else did, but she was eager to eat and get back home. She wanted to see if there was a way for her to check out her aunt's old employees and see what she might be able to learn about them. And she absolutely wasn't going to tell Brett about it yet. "I don't know much, but I'm certain that Drew was not the one who held that knife to my neck. Right now, all I'm sure of is that I want to eat dinner with my friends."

Brett nodded. "You're right. We shouldn't be involving you in any of this." He shared a silent exchange with Brooks.

Brooks went to the grill to help Ruby. "Sounds good, boss. Let's eat."

CHAPTER TEN

Maggie drove home behind Bradley after their quick meal. The news about the death of the young man at the hardware store was enough to dampen their spirits beyond what a friendly bonfire could repair.

"This is so weird, Mom," he said to her after laying Wyatt in his crib for the night. "You just saw that kid. And now he's dead."

"He seemed like a sweetheart, too," Maggie said. "At least, from my brief interaction with him."

"I hope they figure this out soon," he said. "I almost wish we could stay here longer to help keep an eye on you and the donut shop."

Maggie smiled and reached out for her son's arm. "I'll be alright. And the two of you need to get on with your lives. You're a dad now, Bradley. You have

Wyatt and your future to look out for. Besides, I have plenty of eyes on me here."

"I've noticed," he said with a chuckle. "Even so, I wish I could have been there when that guy put a knife to your throat."

"I'm not sure it would have made a difference," she said. "I'm alright. I wasn't hurt, just scared."

"What time are you headed in tomorrow?" Bradley asked her before he went off to bed.

"Probably around seven," Maggie said. "That's when Ruby plans to be there."

"I'll play it by ear with Wyatt, but I will be by a little bit later in the morning," he said.

Maggie left him and retired to her bed. Her sleep was interrupted several times by dreams of tall men sneaking into her bedroom, and the memory of a sharp blade against her neck.

The next morning, she waited for Ruby to show up before she opened her car door to get out. As much as Maggie wanted to play off the incident, she was slowly becoming aware that the intruder had stolen her peace, at least for the time being.

"I'm glad you didn't try to make it inside by yourself," Ruby said when she joined Maggie in the alley. She carried a canvas grocery bag filled with ingredients for breakfast.

"Are you expecting a large crowd?" Maggie laughed at how big the bag was. They moved toward the back door. She slid the key in the lock and waited for a second before she pulled the door open.

"I'm going to set my bag down and the two of us are going to walk through this place together." Maggie noticed the small pistol tucked into Ruby's waistband for the first time.

"You're armed?"

Ruby nodded. "I am well-trained and have a permit for it," she said. "And Brett knows that I planned to carry a firearm this morning."

"Okay," Maggie said. She set the bags containing the doorbell cameras down next to Ruby's bag. "Let's get this over with."

Maggie reached inside and flipped on the lights, just as she had done before. This time, Ruby walked in front of her and checked every corner of the donut shop before she declared the space safe. "Does it make you nervous?" she asked.

"Which part, coming back in here or you carrying a firearm?" Maggie asked.

"Both. Either?" Ruby replied.

Maggie shrugged. "I'm far less nervous than I was five minutes ago," she said. "Let's just leave it at that."

"Well, I guess that's a good thing," Ruby said. She returned to the bag she had left by the door. "I'm going to get started on breakfast. I think everyone should be here within the hour."

"Brett said he and Brooks were both taking the morning off," Maggie said. "I'm assuming Myra and Orson are coming. What about Gretchen? I still feel so bad about how we canceled her delivery for the bed and breakfast."

"It was actually Gretchen who gave me the idea to close up for the day. With everything going on lately, she offered to do something else for the week and since her only guests are Layla and her boyfriend right now, she didn't think it would be too big of a deal." Ruby disappeared into the office for a moment, and then returned without the gun on her hip.

"That was really kind of her, but I'm sad that probably means she can't come by. Anyway, what can I do to help?" she asked.

"Make coffee," she said. "Lots and lots of coffee, and then start some pancake batter, that would help."

Half an hour later, Brooks showed up with Myra, followed by Orson. Bradley arrived right after with Wyatt in tow. Orson moved to the car seat as soon as Bradley set it on one of the tables out front. "Hello, little man," he cooed at the baby. Wyatt rewarded the attention with a slight grasp of his finger.

Brett was the last to arrive. He walked through the back door just as Maggie flipped the last banana pancake from the griddle to the serving platter.

"Where is everybody?" he asked.

"Out front, waiting on you and these pancakes," Maggie said.

"Allow me," Brett said, taking the platter from her. He leaned in for a quick kiss before Maggie opened the swinging door for him and followed him into the front of the donut shop.

The tables had been rearranged in the center of the dining room so they could all fit around it, family-style. "Where do you want these?" Brett asked when he approached the table. Ruby pointed to a space in front of Bradley.

Maggie took her seat next to her son and Brett took the empty chair on the other side of her.

After a moment of awkward silence, Orson tickled Wyatt under his chin. "At least we can be thankful this little one is in a happy mood," he said.

The comment charmed the room and broke the ice. Soon plates were passed, and the comments began about the breakfast and the company.

"What is this, exactly?" Brooks asked after

spooning a generous helping of the egg dish in his mouth.

"Eggs Benedict, with a southern twist," Ruby said with a wink.

"I'm loving these banana pancakes, Mom," Bradley said. "Is this pecan syrup?"

Maggie nodded. "You will be happy to know that these banana pancakes are my only contribution to this gourmet brunch."

"You made the coffee," Myra offered.

"I did." Maggie chuckled.

"Hey, Mom, you are a good cook. A great cook, even," Bradley said. "But it's tough to compete with a professional chef."

"Thanks, I think," Maggie teased.

When breakfast was over, Myra and Orson volunteered to clean up while Brooks and Brett walked around the donut shop with Maggie and Ruby. They started out front where the food truck was parked. Once in a while, a car pulled into the parking lot, looked up at the message on the sign that the donut shop was closed for the day, and then drove on.

Maggie was glad she had opted for a programmable scrolling marquee sign. At least the public could be efficiently notified when the donut shop shut down with little notice. Which hopefully wasn't something that would happen often. Today though, even if she didn't love the idea, she was glad they had closed.

"I still don't know how he got in," Maggie said when the four of them walked together past the front doors.

"You never saw anything out of place or a door or a window ajar?" Brooks asked her. "We didn't find anything that looked out of the ordinary, but sometimes the shop owners' know better or can think of something we don't because of their familiarity."

"Nothing," Maggie said. "And most of these windows are plate glass. There is no opening or closing them."

"The back door wasn't open either," Brett said.

"No, the locksmith had just installed the new lock," Ruby said. "Only the four of us had access to the keys."

"Okay, it doesn't sound like there was an obvious way he came in," Brooks said. "Remind me where you were when he accosted you?"

"I'd just come out of the cooler," Maggie said with a shudder. "I searched the entire place, too. I swear I looked everywhere but still, whoever it was either had to be hiding well or have come in after I looked."

A second later, Ruby walked around the group and stood facing them. "I think I know how he got in," she said at once. She began walking quickly down the sidewalk past the side of the building. She pointed at the two small windows halfway up. "There."

Brett moved directly to the windows and began looking around. He pulled out a pen from his pocket and ran it around the exterior of the window.

"The bathroom windows?" Brooks asked.

Ruby nodded. "That's the men's bathroom," she said.

"The weather stripping around here has been pulled off," Brett said. "And recently. Do you see the difference here?" He pointed to the rubber line he had pulled off.

"What are we looking at?" Ruby asked.

"Dust," Brett replied. "This section here has very little compared to the rest of it. This is why I said that it was recently pulled off. The dust on this length is sticky and thick. But here, this is what he pulled out so he could pop off the screen and slide the window open."

Maggie stared at the window. She could feel the breath of the stranger standing behind her again, and the pressure of the blade on her neck. "How do we stop it?" she asked suddenly. "What can we do to keep him out?"

She felt an arm circle her shoulders and pull her into a sideways hug. "Why don't we head back inside and discuss that very thing?" Brett said. "And then my good buddy Brooks and I can head on over to the hardware store and get to work securing this before the day is over."

Maggie nodded and allowed him to lead her back inside.

CHAPTER ELEVEN

"It was the bathroom?" Bradley asked as soon as they returned to the tables in the middle of the dining room.

"The men's bathroom, specifically," Brooks said. He reached over and took Wyatt gently out of Bradley's arms.

"Hey, man," Bradley said. "You're pretty good at that."

"I'm the oldest of five," Brooks said softly. Wyatt looked up at him as he spoke. "I learned how to change diapers and mix formula before I was seven."

"You already have more experience than I had when this little man was born," Bradley said.

"What are we going to do about those windows, guys?" Orson asked, ready to get down to business.

"Well, that's what we are about to decide," Brett said. "Whatever we do, it needs to happen very quickly."

"Okay, what about bars?" Orson asked.

Brooks shook his head. "I can tell you right now that's not an option."

"Why not? That's how they protect businesses in the city," Orson said.

Maggie wondered which city he meant.

"It's against the fire code here in Dogwood Mountain," Brett said.

"Alright, then what?" Myra asked.

"We can place metal braces inside the windows that will prevent anyone from sliding the windows open," Ruby suggested.

Brett shook his head. "Again, not a good idea if there's a fire," he said. "Honestly, it would be better to replace the windows entirely. We can install more secure windows that open outward for ventilation instead of sliding open. The locks will be more secure, too."

Before Maggie or Ruby could respond, they were surprised by a loud knock at the front door. Maggie looked up at Layla, who was trying her best to open the front door.

"Hold on." Maggie held up a finger, pushed her chair back, and headed for the door.

"I know you're closed," Layla called through the glass. "But I want to see my dad."

Brett was up immediately and joined Maggie at the door. Maggie turned the lock and let the girl in.

"Dad," Layla said first and hugged her father around his middle. "I just wanted to come and see you."

"What's going on?" Brett asked. He pushed her back slightly and studied her face. "You're shaking."

"Dad, it just doesn't make any sense," Layla said.

"What doesn't make sense?" Brett asked her softly. He led her to a chair and sat her down carefully.

"Drew," she said. Maggie noticed the tears rolling down her face for the first time. "There's so much that doesn't make any sense about his death."

"Okay, honey," Brett said. He knelt on the floor in front of her. "I am going to need for you to explain exactly what is going on here."

Layla dropped her head and sighed loudly. She pulled her phone out from her back pocket. "I just found some text messages he sent me," she said. "They must have been from yesterday before he was killed."

"What do those messages say?" Brett carefully

took the phone from her hands and scrolled through the texts. "Brooks?"

At once, Brooks rose from his seat and peered over Brett's shoulder. "Sounds like he was trying to warn you about something," he said.

Layla nodded while a fresh torrent of tears fell. "And I didn't see it because I was too busy with Tommy," she said. "Also, he said something to me that day at the hardware store, too. That day we saw you, Ms. Sharpe."

"It's Maggie, and what did Drew say to you that day, sweetheart?" Maggie asked.

After a deep breath, Layla began her story. "He followed me around the store when I went in there with my mom and Tommy. It was like he was trying to catch me alone," she said. "I got mad at him. I figured he was just jealous. I went away to school, you know. And Drew, he just stayed back here taking online classes and working."

"You thought he was trying to separate you from your boyfriend to win you back or something, right?" Myra asked.

Layla nodded. "I thought he was just jealous of Tommy," she said.

"What made you change your mind?" Myra asked. Maggie was curious, but let the younger woman ask the questions. She seemed to be getting Layla past her tears and able to focus long enough to talk.

"It was the texts," she said. "I just found them this morning. I don't think he finished saying what he wanted to say because the texts seem to cut off in the middle of a sentence."

"Drew was trying to tell you to be careful with all of the robberies taking place," Brett said. "And he mentioned Maggie getting accosted by an intruder."

Layla nodded. "It seemed like he was trying to say that he suspected someone," she said.

"That's what I'm getting from this, too," Brooks agreed. He stood up to his full height.

"Drew wasn't trying to get back together with me," she insisted. "He wrote that he still cared about me as a friend and that he was telling me to be careful like he had told his girlfriend. He seemed worried."

Brett nodded. "He mentioned her in the part of the text message that gets cut off."

"I found her," Layla said. "I looked her up and I went to the bank where she works, and I talked to her. They were dating, and he was concerned about her safety as well as mine. She was already back at work but still so upset about his death."

"Do you think Drew had someone in mind he was

worried about?" Brooks asked.

Layla nodded her head. "I think that's what he was trying to tell me that day at the hardware store," she said. "I should have listened to him."

"Layla, this is very important," Brett said. "Do you think Drew told his girlfriend who he was worried about?"

Layla pursed her lips and seemed lost in thought for a moment. She slowly shook her head and focused her eyes on her father. "No, Dad," she said. "I don't think so. She didn't say anything about anyone specifically."

"Okay, that's good," Brett said. Maggie noted his patience talking with her. "But I am worried that if there was someone he was worried about, they might think Drew already told her. We're going to have someone go and talk to Drew's girlfriend and make sure she is safe. Okay?"

Layla nodded her head again. "Okay, Dad," she said. "I just wish I had listened to him."

Brett patted her leg and stood back up from his kneeling position. "We're going to figure this out. I promise."

CHAPTER TWELVE

Moments later, Maggie heard the door chimes jingle again. Corinne and Steven walked inside the donut shop.

"We're closed, folks," Orson announced gruffly. He glared at Maggie for forgetting to lock the door behind Layla.

Corinne ignored Orson and rushed to her daughter's side. "Why didn't you tell us you were headed over here, Layla? Tommy is out looking for you."

"You had us worried, young lady," Steven added.

Brett's face hardened. "She came here to talk to me," he said. "And she is nineteen."

Maggie stifled a laugh. Not too long ago Brett was acting like Layla was still twelve years old, but now he'd changed his tone.

Steven said nothing but looked Brett up and down as if to size him up. "Even so, you didn't tell anyone you were going anywhere," Corinne said. "What are you all doing here anyway? I thought the donut shop was shut down for the day."

"We are addressing some security concerns," Maggie said, wondering why these people seemed to know so much about her. She knew Dogwood Mountain wasn't the largest town and people talked, but it was getting creepy. Even more so than that, she wanted them to get out so she could find out exactly where Drew's girlfriend worked. She wanted to talk to her on her own and find out what she knew but knew that Brett would want to talk to her first.

"Security concerns? You should have listened to me," Steven said. "I told you I would look into that for you as your insurance agent."

"Thank you, but I have an agent," Maggie said. "And as you can see, I have friends who are experts in the field."

Steven rolled his eyes slightly. "Okay, I'm not going to stop offering, though," he said.

Maggie turned back to Brett. "The windows can wait," she said. "You have more pressing matters to concern yourself with."

"I'll see to the windows," Brooks offered. "I'll let

the chief handle the other situation and we can get these in before the end of the day."

"You'll want to make sure you get the right size," Steven interjected. "Are you sure you have measured correctly? Windows are typically special orders. I swear I don't know why restaurants insist on such odd sizes."

Maggie ignored Steven's constant chatter and excused herself to the back. She had carried the petty cash bag with her when she arrived in case she needed cash for any of the security improvements she anticipated.

When she retrieved the bag, she pulled out cash and returned to the dining room. Steven was still yammering on about security and his expertise in it. Brett had motioned for the two of them to leave and promised to deliver Layla home safely himself.

"I still don't get why you are all gathered around here," Corinne said when they walked out the door. "It's a little weird for a business to shut down for a day just so a group of people can have lunch together."

Maggie watched the pair bicker back and forth as they walked down the sidewalk to their car. Brett led Layla through the kitchen to his car parked in the alley behind the donut shop. "She's something else, isn't she?"

"She's a whole lot of many things," Ruby said. "You didn't know her when she was giving Brett all kinds of heck for having another baby after they divorced."

"Do what?" Orson asked. "What on earth does she have to say about what he and his new wife did after they got divorced?"

"It was something. I swear I have never seen a woman so eager to share every last thought that crosses her mind."

Brett left with his daughter while Myra accompanied Brooks to the hardware store in search of new windows for the bathrooms. Ruby and Maggie worked through a small list of chores they hoped to complete while the donut shop was shut down for a day. While Ruby cleaned the inside of the cooler with bleach and water, Maggie tackled the storeroom. Orson kept them company by pointing out their errors and offering generous advice as needed.

"Can I just say something?" Myra said when they returned from the hardware store with the windows.

"What's that?" Ruby asked. Maggie was busy in the office filing the receipts in the filing cabinet. She made it a point to immediately file anything that might be important for the coming tax season.

"I don't like that Corinne lady, at all," she said. "But that guy she was with? He gives me the heebie-jeebies."

"Steven, for sure," Maggie agreed. "He's way too cocky for my tastes, but it's Layla's boyfriend that really weirds me out. He's always next to her and clearly wasn't happy about Drew and their past relationship."

"I don't care much for Steven, either," Brooks said. "I have to admit, though, everyone in the group seems rather off."

"By the way, have you heard from Brett at all?" Maggie asked.

Brooks shook his head. "Hopefully not much longer. I'm going to the restroom to see what I can do about these windows. I'll let you know if I hear from him."

"It's like you all have some sort of psychic connection," Ruby said no more than two minutes later. "Brett's back."

Maggie dried her hands on a dishtowel and joined Ruby by the door.

"How's Layla?" Maggie asked when Brett walked back through the back door without her.

"She went off with her boyfriend." Brett rolled his eyes.

"What happened with the girlfriend?" Maggie asked, so eager for the answer she rocked back and forth on her heels.

"She never came back to work after her break," Brett said. His face seemed frozen in a permanent frown. "Where's Brooks?"

"He's in the men's room with Myra trying to take the old window out. Hey, Brett," she called to him before he went off to find Brooks. "Forgive me for asking so many questions, but why did Layla leave with Tommy? If you ask me, he might be someone you all should be worried about."

Brett sighed and dropped his head. "We stopped off at the bank before I dropped her off. Corinne called while we were on our way there," he said. "And then the boyfriend showed up and convinced her that she was overreacting, so she left. I can't tell you how thankful I am that Layla is the only one in that group that's close to me. They're all driving me crazy."

"But why would you let her leave with him?" Maggie asked.

"It wasn't just him. Corinne and Steven came too. They all just traipsed in the bank like it was nothing.

I'm not a fan of my ex-wife, but I have to trust that she wouldn't let anything happen to Layla while they were together. And it seems none of these people can go anywhere alone."

He suddenly blew past them and headed for the dining room. Ruby cast a sideways look at Maggie and shrugged her shoulders.

"I guess we need to leave that alone for now," Maggie said.

"I'm worried about this girl," Ruby said.

"Maybe we should leave things alone for now, but I am worried about the girl, too," Maggie admitted. She inhaled deeply herself and placed her hands on her hips. "I'm going to ask Myra for her name then I'm going to look into her for myself."

"Why ask Myra?"

"Because she talks to Brooks," Maggie said. "And I think Brett is distracted with whatever is going on with Layla."

"You know how he is going to feel about you asking questions," Ruby said. "Even though we have all sat around figuring things out before, I think this time is different. Not only is his daughter involved, but his girlfriend's shop was broken into twice and one of those times she was attacked... In case you forgot, I mean."

Maggie gave her the side-eye. "Either way, I'm going to find out her name and I'm going to warn her that Drew was worried about someone. She deserves to know. And what if… what if she worked for the donut shop before? What if it was her who did all this? Maybe she and Drew were fighting about something, and she killed him and tried to frame him? I know I said this same thing about Drew's boss, but Ruby, this girl didn't come back to work. It might be because she's in mourning, but we've seen our fair share of bad people. It could also be because she's in hiding from murdering her boyfriend."

"Were you able to find anything about old employees?" Ruby asked. Maggie knew she was avoiding her tirade about Drew's girlfriend being the robber and killer simply because she was a woman and Maggie had made it clear that she's heard a man's voice. And she had, but stranger things had happened.

"I found a list, but so much has been going on, I haven't exactly been able to go around town to all the places that got hit to see if any of those people might have worked there too." Maggie frowned.

"Ever think about passing that list to Brett?"

"Yes, but not yet."

Ruby shook her head and got back to work.

CHAPTER THIRTEEN

Lauren Cooper was nowhere to be found when Maggie made the bank deposit the following day. She deliberately chose to walk the deposit into the bank and look for her. After getting her name from Myra, she compared it to the old employee list from her aunt, and didn't find anything comparable, but she still wanted to check in on her.

"Lauren no longer works here," the thin-lipped bank manager told her when she asked.

"That's funny," Maggie said, feigning confusion. "I was just here recently, and she was working."

"Well, that's what happens when you are a no call, no show," the manager snapped.

"Has anyone checked on her? There have been a

lot of weird things happening around town," Maggie said.

"Is it my job to go to the house of each one of my employees when they decide to ditch work? I don't think so," he said.

"Given the fact that her boyfriend was just found dead, I would think you might show a little bit of concern." Maggie picked up her receipt and bank bag and marched straight out the door to her car.

"Lauren Cooper didn't show up for work today or yesterday," she said to Ruby from her car. "The manager was pretty rude about me asking."

"I'm not that surprised," Ruby said. "Are you heading back here soon?"

"I'll be there in five minutes," Maggie said and shut off her phone. She drove through town but turned down the residential street she found online as Lauren's last known address. When she got to the address in the middle of the block, she found an average-looking duplex with a twenty-year-old Toyota parked outside of the first unit. Maggie parked her car on the street and walked up to the first unit. She knocked on the door and waited. The door was on the inside above the single garage below. The unit next door appeared to be a mirror of it. Both front doors were close together.

No one answered after the first knock. Maggie leaned into the door slightly and tried to listen for sounds of movement inside.

When she heard nothing, she knocked more firmly and waited again. She leaned over to the left and peered into the window. Broken mini blinds covered most of the window, but she could see a cluttered kitchen and dining area through the slats. The lights were off, and the place appeared to be empty.

She moved to the second unit and knocked again. This time, the front windows were covered by drapes. Maggie knocked a second time but heard nothing, aside from the deep meow of a cat on the other side of the door. She turned to walk back down the steep concrete steps to her car.

When she was halfway down the steps, Maggie looked down the street.

She spotted a dark green Jeep Cherokee parked two houses down from where she stood. She could see someone in the driver's seat and the engine was idling. At first, Maggie shrugged it off. Anyone could park out on the street, but the sight of the vehicle and someone sitting inside it made the hair on the back of her neck stand up.

When she returned to her car, her phone was ringing. For a second, her heart sank when she realized that she had left her phone in the car while she was knocking on the doors of the strange duplex. All the while, she had thought the phone was in her back pocket.

"Hello," she said when she answered.

"You said you would be here in five minutes," Ruby said. "This isn't the time to scare me like that."

"I stopped by that address I found for Lauren," Maggie said.

"Alone? And you didn't tell anyone," Ruby asked. "What were you thinking?"

"I was thinking that I would go and check on her," Maggie said. She decided it wasn't a good time to mention that she had left the phone in her car. She started her car and sat for a moment. The green Jeep pulled away from the curb and turned around in a neighboring driveway, and then drove down the street in the opposite direction. Maggie exhaled relief.

"Well, get here as fast as you can," Ruby said. "That was not part of the plan, but I want to know everything."

"I'm headed in," Maggie said. She backed out of the drive and headed back to the main road.

She drove two blocks and spotted the green Jeep again, this time it turned off of a side street and fell in behind her.

Once again, Maggie's senses told her that something was off. She passed the turn to the donut shop and headed for the Dogwood Mountain Police Department. As soon as the police station came into view, the Jeep veered right and took off on another side street. Maggie pulled to a stop in front of the police station. She drummed her fingers on the steering wheel and considered going inside.

But there was no real threat, and she had no proof that the run-in with the Jeep was anything more than a coincidence in a small town.

"You sure are bent on giving me a heart attack today," Ruby said when Maggie returned to the donut shop. "I have been beside myself waiting for you to get back here."

"Sorry. One thing keeps leading to another." She told Ruby about finding nothing at Lauren's house but left out the Jeep for the time being.

"It's okay that you didn't find her, you know."

Maggie pulled her apron back off of the hook by the office door and tied it behind her waist. "I guess. But someone did this and it's time to find out who it was."

"I don't know about you sometimes." She shook her head. "We don't always have to be the people who find things out. I know I go along with you all the time, but this isn't the same, Maggie. You could have been killed yourself. This one feels way too close to home."

"Well, I'm here and I'm okay and since I don't know any more about anything than I did yesterday, we might as well just get to work. Where do you need me?"

Ruby sighed and digressed. "I think we need some vanilla and blueberry scones, but that's it. I've got everything else already set aside for the boxed lunches. And the display case is still full."

"Are we slow today?" Maggie asked. She chastised herself for not paying more attention to the flow of business.

"Maybe a little." Ruby turned away from the prep table and faced Maggie.

"Another business got hit early this morning. I don't think very many people are in a hurry to come out today."

"Another business? What is that, two since Drew was killed?" Maggie asked. "What business was hit?"

"Here is the scary part," Ruby said. "It was a beauty salon over on Fourth Street, not a typical business. The place was just some converted garage a lady cut hair in right next to her house."

"Oh, my gosh." Maggie felt the hairs on her neck

stand up again. "Was the woman there? Was she hurt?"

"Not her, but an employee," she said. "A young shampoo girl was there to open up. The intruder had a mask and made threats, but he didn't actually hurt her."

"I guess that officially clears Drew," Maggie said. She turned back to the scones.

"Myra said Brooks was called into Brett's office along with a handful of other officers," Ruby said quietly. "I think the police are starting to get pretty serious about these robberies."

"Robberies? How about robberies, one stick up at knifepoint, and also that little issue with Drew's death," Maggie said. She could hear the acidity in her tone, but she was unfazed. "And now they want to form some sort of a task force? What about Lauren Cooper? Brett gets distracted over his feelings about his daughter's boyfriend, so he stops worrying about her?"

"I'm not sure that's fair, Maggie," Ruby said. "We've all been taken by surprise over the past few days."

Maggie sighed. "I agree that it has been a bit of a shock, but this is not the first time this police department has had to investigate a death."

"No, but there are some extenuating circumstances," Ruby said.

Maggie pulled the towel off of the scones and began pressing her fingertips into the dough to form a circle. "I want to check out Lauren's social media again after this," she said. "I want to see if there are any places she might have gone off to, like a friend or her mom's house or something. Maybe we can even find something that might link her to whoever could have done this. We always seem to find pictures online or something someone posted about that leads to the answer we are looking for."

"I think I will mention this to Brooks as well," Ruby said. "I don't want to mess around too much on our own. She could be missing. Or she could have absolutely nothing to do with this. I'm honestly thinking this has nothing to do with her at all and it's all about Layla's boyfriend. That explains why Brett's so distracted. He might think so too."

"There was a Jeep," Maggie said slowly. She was sure that she was going to sound paranoid and ridiculous, but Ruby already seemed a bit cautious about what was going on and she hated to keep things from her friend.

"What Jeep, and where?"

"It was parked down the street from the duplex

where Lauren lives. Someone was in it, and it was running while I was there. I swear there was someone in it watching me," Maggie said. "But it took off when I got back down to my car."

"Did it follow you?" Ruby asked.

"Not until I was driving back in this direction," Maggie said. "They seemed a little aggressive, so I drove by the police station, and they took off in another direction."

"Did you see who was inside? Any idea if it was male or female?"

Maggie began cutting the scones into triangles. "Honestly, I don't know if they were following me. And yes, I think based on the height and build of the driver's silhouette that it was a man, or at least a very tall woman. I don't know if I am just overreacting about it or not."

"I don't think we can be too careful." Ruby dried her hands off on a towel by the sink and began placing boxed lunches on a tray. She suddenly froze. "You may think this is crazy, but isn't Corinne kind of a very tall woman?"

Maggie felt a lump form in her throat. She quickly worked out the details in her head. Corinne was, in fact, a very tall woman. It might not explain the man's voice she'd heard, and it was hard to tell if she didn't like Drew or was just hateful about everything in her life. But if she didn't want her daughter to be with Drew, then trying to frame him and then killing him, could be a solution. A bad one, but a solution, nonetheless. She wondered if maybe the situations weren't related at all. What if the robber had nothing to do with Drew?

She told Ruby her thoughts and waited for a reply that might help clear things up.

"I have to take these up front really quick," she said. "Why don't you put those scones in the oven and take a look at Lauren's online profile again. Then we can go from there."

"You mean, you're not going to tell me to let this go?"

"Not entirely," Ruby said. She placed the last two boxes on the tray and headed to the swinging door. "But I think at least one of our law enforcement friends needs to know what we figure out."

"If we figure anything out…" Maggie said after Ruby left the kitchen.

CHAPTER FOURTEEN

"The chief didn't mention anything more about Lauren Cooper," Brooks told Maggie and Ruby over lunch the next day. "I know he was going there yesterday at some point to check up on things, but I don't know what happened afterward."

"He must not be too concerned over her where-abouts then," Maggie said. She wanted to add that she was glad Brett hadn't run into her when she was there, but kept her mouth shut.

"If he is, it isn't something he brought up to me," Brooks said. "In the meantime, why don't you fill me in on what you know, and I will see what I can figure out."

Maggie relayed the incident with the manager at

the bank. "It seems as if Lauren hasn't shown up for work in two days," she said.

"Give me a second," Brooks said. He turned away with his cell phone for a moment.

"You should tell him about the Jeep," Ruby urged Maggie.

"What Jeep?" Myra asked. She had remained quiet for most of the conversation.

"Maggie checked on an address where Lauren may have been living and there was a Jeep parked outside and running," Ruby said. "It might have been watching her. And it followed a few minutes later."

"Hold up," Brooks said when he rejoined the conversation. "What is this about a Jeep?"

Maggie repeated what she had told Myra and Ruby, "I don't even know if it is relevant," she said.

"What color was this Jeep?" Brooks asked.

"A dark green," Maggie said. "And it wasn't brand new, either."

"How old was it, would you say?" Brooks asked. Maggie noted a new urgency in his questions that she hadn't heard before.

"Maybe fifteen years old," Maggie said. "I'm not very good at dating cars, but this one still had some of the boxy shape to it. It didn't look like all of the other SUVs I see everywhere."

"Hold that thought for just a second," Brooks said. He put up his index finger and stepped away with his phone again.

"I wonder what's going on?" Maggie whispered to Ruby and Myra.

"We're about to find out," Myra said when Brooks hung up his phone and stared briefly at the wall behind them. "That's his heavy concentration face."

Brooks hung his phone up for the second time and turned back to Maggie. "Can you try to give me a detailed description of the vehicle? I need to know absolutely everything you can remember about it, where it went, what you could see of the driver, and when they started following you," he said.

"Sure," Maggie answered as a few customers came in the shop. "Let's go back to my office."

Brooks followed her to the back and took notes while she described the vehicle once more. "What can you tell me about the driver?" Brooks asked.

"Not much," Maggie said. "As I told you, I didn't get a very good look at whoever it was."

"Okay, but when you did look into the Jeep for the first time, was the driver's head higher than the steering wheel?"

Maggie thought for a moment. "Yes, for sure."

"So, would you say the driver's shoulders were even with the back of the seat?" Brooks asked.

Maggie nodded. "I think so," she said. "I think that's why I thought it was a man and not a woman. But I can't be sure," she added, still worried about Corinne but not quite ready to accuse Brett's ex-wife of anything.

"Good, good," Brooks said. He pulled his phone out again and typed in a text message. A second later, the phone alerted him to a reply.

Brooks studied the screen for a second and then turned it around to show Maggie. "Is this the vehicle?"

"Yes, it is." She nodded frantically. "How did you know? Have they found the vehicle?"

"You might say that," Brooks said. "Brett just arrested Tommy Pogue for burglary, assault with a deadly weapon, and the murder of Drew Lee."

"Ruby was right!"

"It seems so," he said. "He needs you to go down to the station as soon as you can and make a statement."

"Me?"

"Yes, Maggie," he said. "The assault charge stems from the attack on you, here at the donut shop."

Maggie followed Brooks back out into the dining

room. As she walked, her heart sank lower and lower. She pictured the young man smiling a few days ago when he appeared at her donut shop with Layla. It was the first time she had met either one and the first of Brett's kids she had met. Both seemed so sure of themselves and their time off from school. But now, he sat in a jail cell facing devastating charges, including murder. It made sense, though. He was jealous of Drew.

"The timing just doesn't fit right," she said aloud.

"What? Did you say something?" Ruby asked. Brooks rejoined Myra to say goodbye while Ruby and Maggie looked over the remaining donuts in the display case.

She turned around and whispered, "Brooks said that Tommy was arrested for the murder of Drew Lee."

"Tommy?" Ruby raised a brow. "It's like I've been saying that from the beginning or something…"

"Funny. But something just feels off about this. Like, the timing I was just thinking about."

"What timing?"

"Well." Maggie leaned against the display case and spoke in hushed tones, "If Drew was trying to warn Layla about someone, and that person was

Tommy, what was he trying to say to me in the hardware store?"

"I don't follow," Ruby admitted.

Maggie hung her head for a moment. "That happened just hours after Layla showed up in town with Tommy for the first time and announced that they were taking time off of school and living together, remember?"

"Right, at the food truck that morning was the first time Brett found out as well."

"Yeah, and I think that's pretty much when they first got to town," Maggie said. "Probably the night before, because of what Orson said about Gretchen being busy with the kids, but not days before or anything."

"You might need to make a phone call," Ruby suggested.

"A phone call? To the jail?"

"No, to the Dogwood House," Ruby said. "You need to ask Gretchen when her young guests first arrived."

"I'm going to the police station first," Maggie replied, surprising everyone.

CHAPTER FIFTEEN

Maggie started her car and before she could protest, Ruby opened the passenger door and got in.

"Let's go, Thelma." She clapped her hand on the dash. "I'll call Gretchen on the way."

"You got it, Louise." Maggie pointed the car out of the alley and headed for the police station while Ruby made the call.

"Brett is waiting for you." Brooks texted her when she parked her car in the Dogwood Mountain Police Department parking lot. "You should go right on in."

Maggie pulled the keys from the ignition and headed straight in with Ruby right at her side. She had a one track mind and couldn't wait to talk to Brett.

"Look at all of the people in the waiting room," Ruby whispered when they reached the front doors.

"It's Corinne and her boyfriend," Maggie replied quietly.

"Go right on in," Officer Ruiz said when she appeared behind them. "Just head back to Brett's office and speak with him."

Maggie nodded and headed inside. She and Ruby veered through the waiting area and headed past the small group of people.

"I want to speak with my daughter," Corinne shouted. "She is not under arrest! I want to speak with my daughter!"

"Ma'am, I need for you to calm down right now," Officer Ruiz said. Ruby and Maggie continued past them.

"Wait, wait," Corinne shouted. "Where is she going? Why does the donut lady get to go back there, and I have to stay here? That's my daughter back there! What is wrong with you people? Just because she's dating the help, doesn't mean she should get special treatment. I sure never did…"

"Ms. Sharpe is a witness in a pending case, and so is your daughter," Officer Ruiz told her, standing in her way.

"Just keep moving along," Ruby whispered. "Ignore her."

They reached the hall just outside his office. "Brett," Maggie called out.

"In here," Brett called back. "Come on in and shut the door."

"Do you want me to wait out here?" Ruby asked.

"No, you're part of this, too," he said.

Ruby closed the door and moved further into the small office. Layla was seated in a chair in the corner. Her eyes were puffy, and her face was streaked with tears.

"It wasn't him, Daddy." Layla sobbed softly. "I swear he isn't a killer."

"There is no 'daddy' in here, sweetheart," Brett said. "I have to follow the evidence. This is a very serious matter."

"I understand that it is a serious matter," Layla huffed. "But he's only twenty years old. His life is in the balance here."

"Brett," Maggie cut in. "Brooks said that you wanted to see me."

"Yes, I'm sorry," Brett apologized. He gestured toward two chairs crowded close to the door. "Please have a seat."

Maggie and Ruby took their seats. "You should know that we just talked to Gretchen LeClair. Based on the time Layla and Tommy checked into the bed and breakfast, I don't think Drew would have had known Tommy long enough to form any suspicions about him."

"What does that mean?" Layla asked. "I told you we had two rooms. We would have stayed with Mom and Steven, but they only have a one bedroom house and…"

"Just a minute," Brett interrupted her. He focused on Maggie. "Why did you call Gretchen?"

"Because it dawned on me that for Drew to have texted Layla and Lauren about someone he was suspicious about, he had to know them," Maggie said. "And he didn't have time to know him."

"But he knew Tommy and Layla were dating," Brett admitted. "Corinne and Layla both told me that already. He might not have known him personally, but if he was jealous of Drew for any reason, then what?"

"All I know is what my gut tells me, and Gretchen is on her way down here now to give you a statement," Maggie said. She didn't know if it was Tommy or not, and she knew cops couldn't go by her gut feelings alone, but she was more apt to believe it was Corinne herself, or maybe both Corinne and Steven together. She didn't like either one of them one bit, but she wasn't so sure about mentioning that in front of Layla. Accusing her boyfriend's ex-wife of robbery and murder probably wasn't the best way to win her over.

"Okay, well, we'll get her statement when she comes down," Brett said. He turned to Ruby. "I suppose you'd like to make a statement about this too?"

Ruby nodded. She had no time to speak before they heard a noise in the hallway outside of the office.

"Stay here," Brett warned. He stood and threw the door open. "What is going on out here?"

"I told these people that I want to speak with my daughter," Corinne said. She shoved past Brett and pushed her way into the office. "Honey, are you okay? I'm going to call our attorney!"

Steven was close on her heels. He pushed past Corinne and stood beside Layla. "You're going to leave here right now," he said and pulled her up by her arm.

"Ouch, you're hurting me," Layla said. "Please let go of my arm."

"Just be quiet and head this way," Steven said. "You aren't under arrest, and you don't need to be here."

"Stop it!" Brett said. "Let her go. She is just a witness and not a suspect. There is no need for lawyers and believe it or not, I know a little about the law."

"I'm taking my daughter out of here." Corinne glared at Brett. "You have no right to hold her just because that old ex-boyfriend of hers wound up dead. I told you for years that he was a good for nothing and was just going to cause trouble for her. Even after Layla left, it didn't matter. The kid lies, cheats, steals, and was apparently so caught up in whatever mess he'd created that he got himself killed. What, Mr. Police Officer, you didn't think to look further into all the places that were robbed? Maybe it was one of these small-town business owners that Drew promised to help with their security systems, but really he was too busy casing the place to actually do anything helpful and he got caught. You need to let our daughter leave here right this instant and maybe you should tell your girlfriend to get out too so you can do some actual police work. Come on Layla," she said, holding her hand out. "We'd better get out of here before your father accuses me next."

"She's not going anywhere," Brett said. "She is over eighteen and a material witness in an ongoing investigation." Maggie was surprised at his calm and resolve. "And if you don't calm down, you won't be going anywhere either."

"Let me go," Layla shouted again. Everyone had been so enthralled by Corinne's rant that they'd stopped looking at Steven. "I am not leaving. I'm here to give my statement and help get Tommy out of jail. He didn't do this!"

"Get Tommy out of jail? Why would you want to do that?" Steven asked. He didn't relax his grip on Layla's arm. "I told you he was a bad guy. It seems you're always picking the bad ones."

"You never said a word about him," Layla protested. She yanked her arm away from him, but Steven held tight.

Brett eyed Steven's grip on his daughter's arm. His hand moved slowly to the pistol on his hip. "You better remove your hand from my daughter right now."

"Fine," Steven said. "But you need to let her leave here. She's obviously very upset by all of this."

"I don't think you need to coach me on how to deal with my daughter," Brett said. "Corinne, you are interrupting an investigation. I can't have you back here raising a fuss while I am trying to question these witnesses."

"Witnesses," Steven scoffed. He shook his head. "What can the local donut maker tell you? She didn't even know well enough to hire me as her agent. That's gotta tell you something."

Maggie cast a sideways look in Ruby's direction. Steven stepped toward Layla again. Maggie saw his hand tighten on Layla's arm again. He leaned in and whispered to her.

"Stop it," Layla shouted. "Leave me alone, Steven!"

"I told you to shut up," Steven growled. Maggie stiffened.

"That's him," she said softly. She turned to Steven. "It's you."

Slowly, she became aware of Brett's gun leaving his hip. Steven grabbed Layla and pushed her in front of him. "You'd better not," he warned.

"What are you doing?" Corinne shrieked and hit Steven on his arm. Without looking in her direction he knocked her to the side with his free hand.

"Come here," Ruby said quietly. She reached down and helped Corinne up and moved her across the room. "You need to let Brett handle this."

Steven turned to Maggie. "You, get over here," he ordered.

"Shut up," Brett ordered. "Get your hands of Layla and put them in the air."

"Not happening," Steven said.

"Hold on," Maggie said. "If I come over there, will you let Layla go? She can't testify to what I can."

Steven eyed her for a long second. He seemed to consider her offer, but he took too long. Layla dropped to her knees and knocked him off his balance. Before Maggie could exhale, he was on the ground with his hands behind his back and Brett's knee on his spine.

CHAPTER SIXTEEN

"Okay, this is the part where you give us all the juicy details," Myra said. They sat together around the bonfire once more in front of Ruby's barn, Bradley rocking a sleepy baby Wyatt. It was their last night in town for a while and everyone was glad to be spending it with friends and family. Even Layla was there, in the seat next to her father. However, after his release, Tommy had decided he belonged back home in his childhood bedroom in his parents' home. Maggie couldn't blame him. She was all too aware of the toll of being accused of murder could have on an innocent young man.

"I think it was fairly self-explanatory when he manhandled my daughter," Brett said.

"Oh, sorry, Chief." Myra giggled. "I was talking to Maggie."

Brett's face colored slightly. He threw his arms over his head and turned to Maggie. "Okay, oh Great Detective." He smirked. "Perhaps you can fill us in on how you solved this crime."

"I'll admit that I was pretty sure it had to have been an ex-employee of the donut shop who also worked at some of the other shops. It made no sense to me how the robber would know where to look for our petty cash bag and iPads, but the more that I think about it now, the more it makes sense that with all the 'I'm the best agent in the world crap' from Steven, it was pretty likely that he'd been inside a small business or two over the course of his career. He's a lot of things, but dumb isn't one of them."

"And don't forget his voice," Ruby began. "The way your body clenched when you heard him whisper so gruffly to Layla. You guys, I'm telling you, the moment she heard it, Maggie just knew."

"I have to admit something else," Maggie said, looking around at the group. "I kind of thought Corinne might have been in on it, too." Her eyes were torn between Brett and Layla.

"Maggie!" Brett hid his smile from Layla, but everyone else saw it.

"No, Dad. She's not wrong. Mom was being super weird. She wouldn't leave Steven's side and neither one of them would leave me and Tommy alone. But it wasn't about him or us, it was about you guys."

"Who guys?" Brett asked.

"You and Maggie. After you told me about your relationship, I let it slip to Mom. You know she never likes it when you find someone new. Some of your other choices in women weren't all that great, but I like Maggie, and I think that made Mom mad and I know it made Steven mad to know Mom was jealous. She was so obvious. Everything was such a mess and I feel terrible about all of it."

"The guy didn't do a very good job of covering his tracks once he was under the microscope," Brooks said. "And Maggie was right, Steven knew where to look for things. Not only did he admit to going there the first time because he was upset about how concerned Corinne was about Maggie and Brett, but he admitted to going back the second time just to scare her. He was so mad that she dismissed him about her insurance needs, that he couldn't help himself."

"Of course, he didn't admit any of that to my face," Brett rolled his eyes. "He made it very clear he was only willing to talk to Brooks."

"I think it was only a matter of time, anyway," Layla chimed in. "I think we would have seen through his facade sooner or later. I mean, look at how he loved Tommy one minute, and then threw him under the bus the next. Beyond that, though, you mentioned him being mad Maggie didn't want to hire him, he hated rejection. Of course, he broke in to all the places that rejected him. He wanted business and wasn't getting it."

"Very impressive, young lady." Ruby grinned. "You have the makings of a good detective yourself."

"Well, I hope so," she said and took her father's hand. "Because I have decided to go back to school."

"You have? Oh, honey, that's great." Brett smiled. He reached over to hug her and paused for a moment. "Are you sure, even after all this going on? You can take a little more time if you need it."

Maggie smiled, enjoying seeing Brett be so fatherly.

"I think it's a good plan no matter how she gets to it," Bradley said. "You never know what life is going to throw at you. Get your degree while you can." On cue, Wyatt fussed in his arms.

"Well, I'm sure, but that's not all," Layla said when her father released her from his embrace. "I've changed my major, too. I think it is the most adult thing I have ever done."

"What did you change it to?" Maggie asked.

Layla looked at her father for a long moment and then answered, "Criminal Justice. I talked to Lauren again this morning and after hearing everything she had to say, I just knew. All of a sudden, I knew what I wanted to do with my life. I want to help people."

Orson held up a hand as though he was asking for permission to speak. "That's great, Layla. But I have to ask, are you planning on sticking around here in Dogwood Mountain or what?"

"I'm not sure yet, why?" she asked.

"Well, I already have my hands full with all the other…" He eyed Maggie. "Detectives around here. I'm not sure I can handle another."

***

If you enjoyed A Hidden Jam, check out the next book in the series, Knead 'Em and Weep, today!

AUTHOR'S NOTE

I'd love to hear your thoughts on my books, the story-lines, and anything else that you'd like to comment on —reader feedback is very important to me. My contact information, along with some other helpful links, is listed on the next page. If you'd like to be on my list of "folks to contact" with updates, release and sales notifications, etc.... just shoot me an email and let me know. Thanks for reading!

Also…

… if you're looking for more great reads, Summer Prescott Books publishes several popular series by outstanding Cozy Mystery authors.

CONTACT SUMMER PRESCOTT BOOKS PUBLISHING

Blog and Book Catalog: http://summerprescottbooks.com
Email: summer.prescott.cozies@gmail.com

And…be sure to check out the Summer Prescott Cozy Mysteries fan page and Summer Prescott Books Publishing Page on Facebook – let's be friends!

To sign up for our fun and exciting newsletter, which will give you opportunities to win prizes and swag, enter contests, and be the first to know about New Releases, click here: http://summerprescottbooks.com

Made in United States
North Haven, CT
15 March 2023

34103787R00075